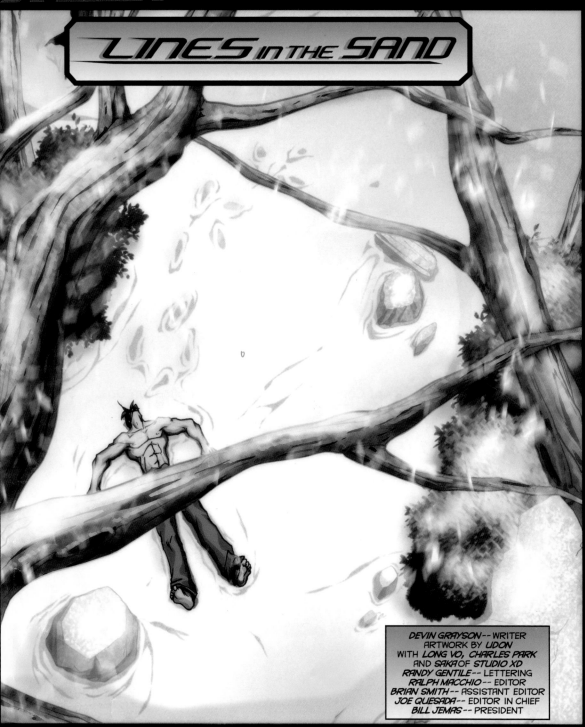

X-MEN: EVOLUTION

LINES IN THE SAND

DEVIN GRAYSON -- WRITER
ARTWORK BY UDON
WITH LONG VO, CHARLES PARK
AND SAKAI OF STUDIO XD
RANDY GENTILE -- LETTERING
RALPH MACCHIO -- EDITOR
BRIAN SMITH -- ASSISTANT EDITOR
JOE QUESADA -- EDITOR IN CHIEF
BILL JEMAS -- PRESIDENT

VISIT US AT
www.abdopub.com

Spotlight, a division of ABDO Publishing Company Inc., is the school and library distributor of the Marvel Entertainment books.

Library bound edition © 2006

Library of Congress Cataloging-in-Publication Data

Lines In the Sand

ISBN 1-59961-054-X   (Reinforced Library Bound Edition)

All Spotlight books are reinforced library binding and manufactured in the United States of America

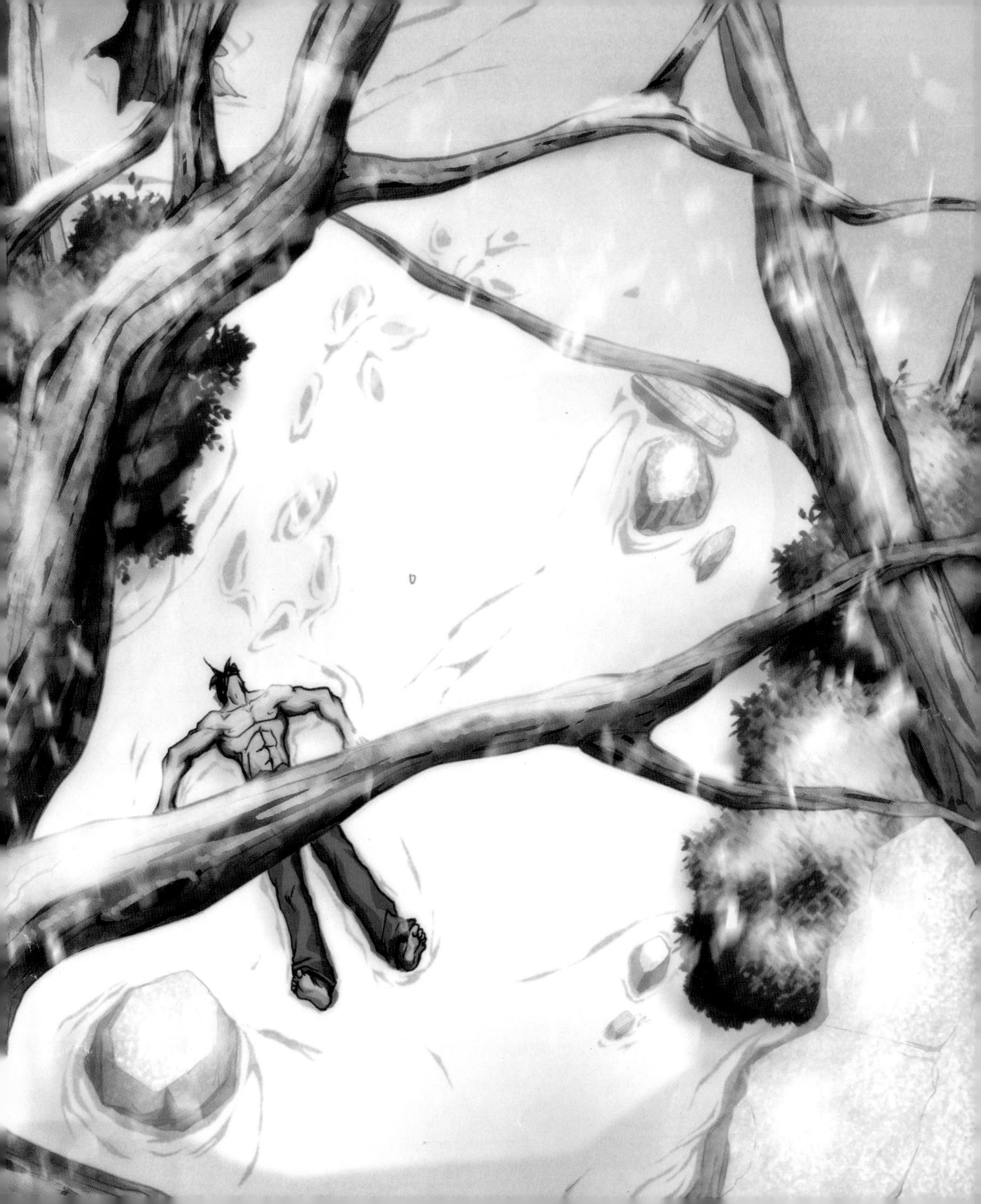

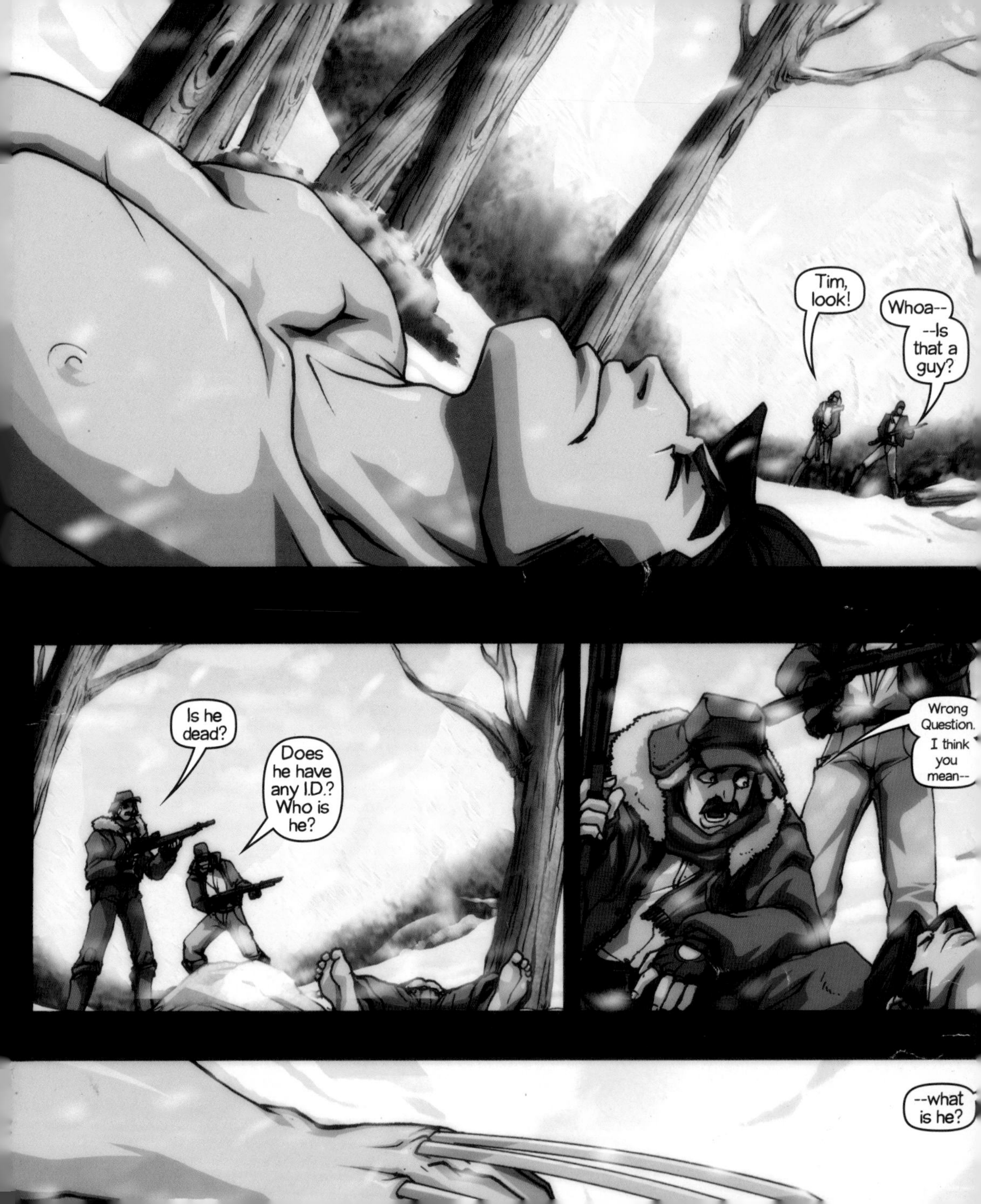

Tim, look!
Whoa--
--Is that a guy?
Is he dead?
Does he have any I.D.? Who is he?
Wrong Question. I think you mean--
--what is he?

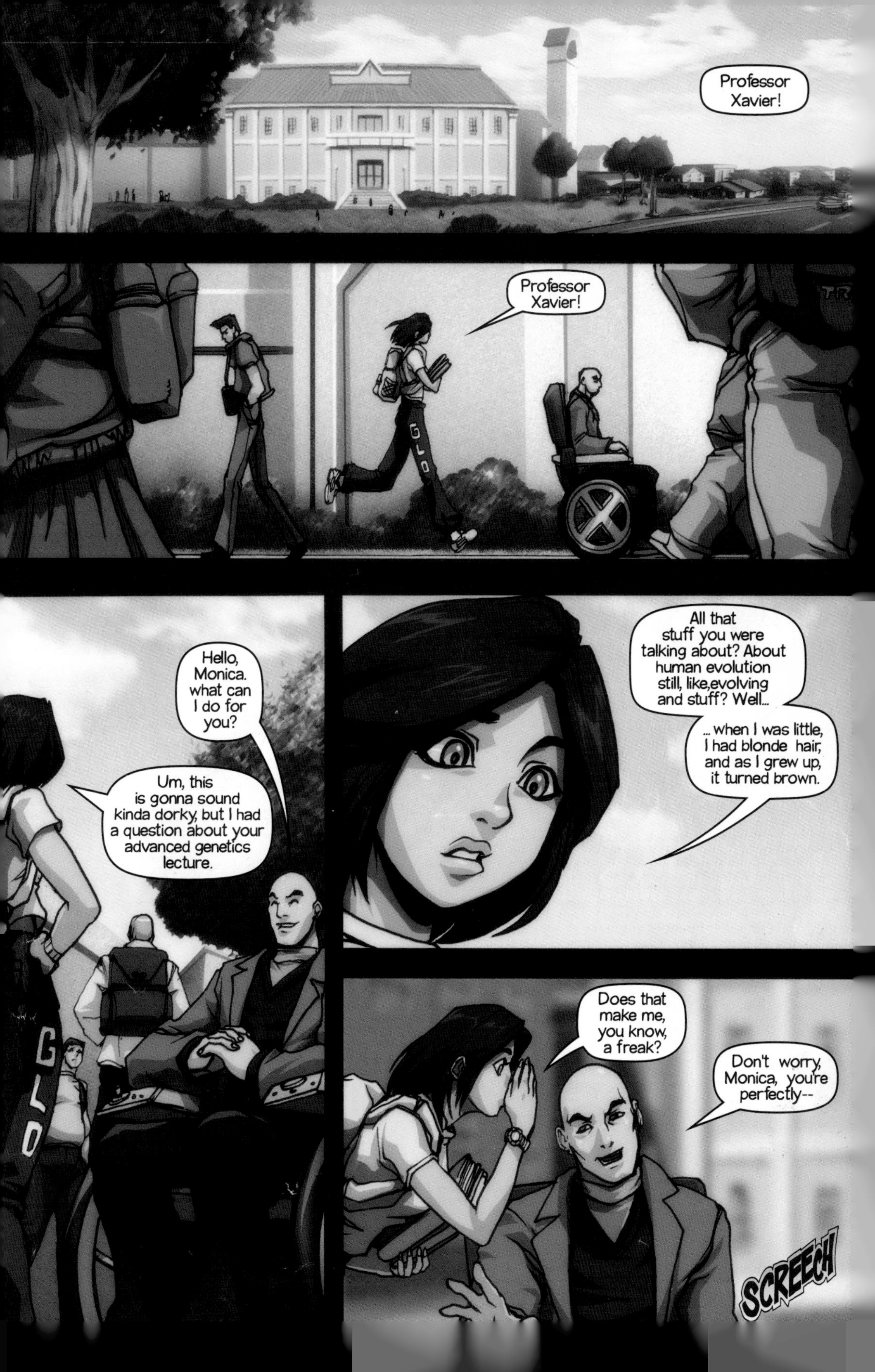
Professor Xavier!
Professor Xavier!
Hello, Monica. what can I do for you?
Um, this is gonna sound kinda dorky, but I had a question about your advanced genetics lecture.
All that stuff you were talking about? About human evolution still, like,evolving and stuff? Well...
...when I was little, I had blonde hair, and as I grew up, it turned brown.
Does that make me, you know, a freak?
Don't worry, Monica, you're perfectly--
SCREECH

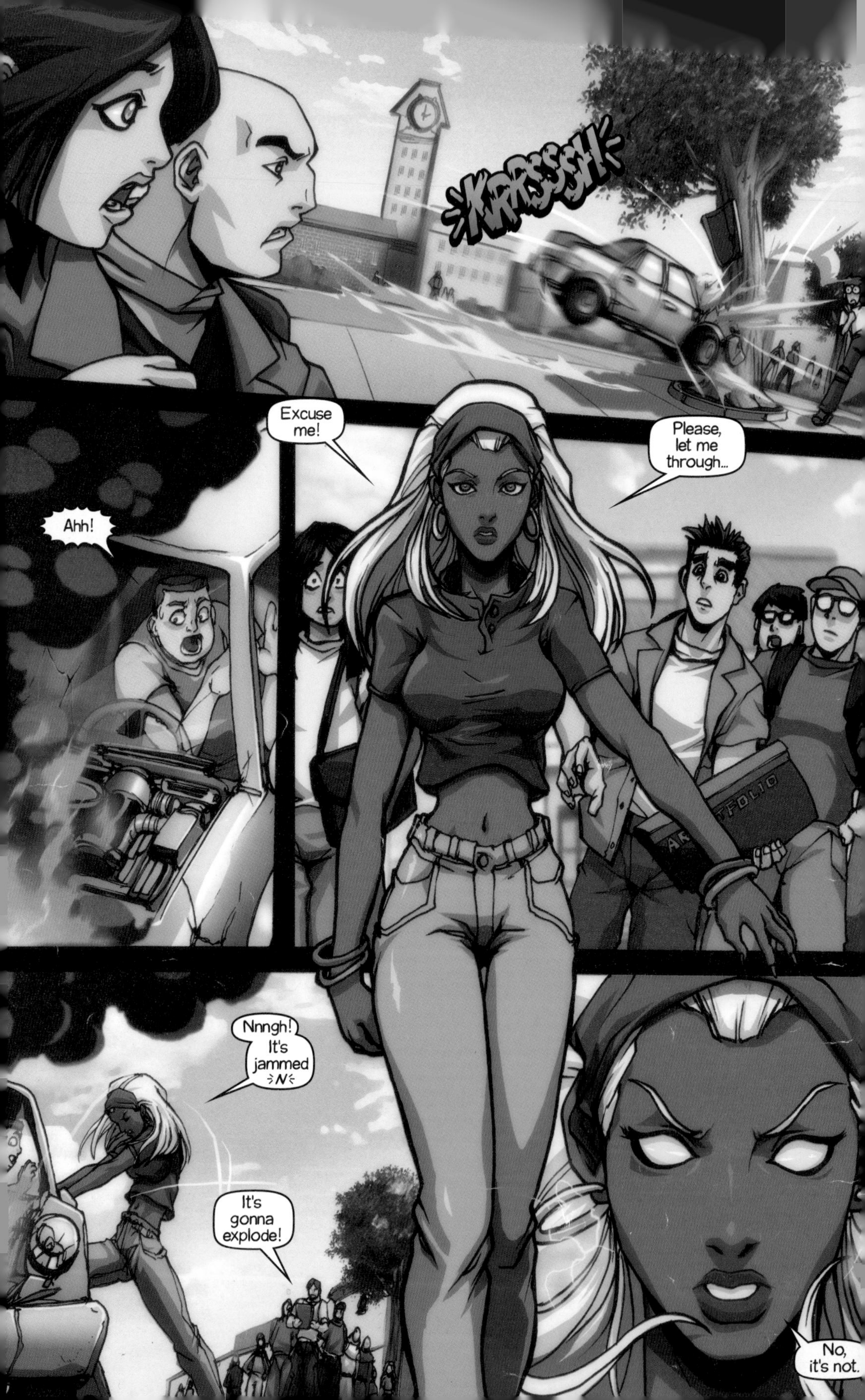
KRRSSSH
Excuse me!
Please, let me through...
Ahh!
Nnngh! It's jammed
N
It's gonna explode!
No, it's not.

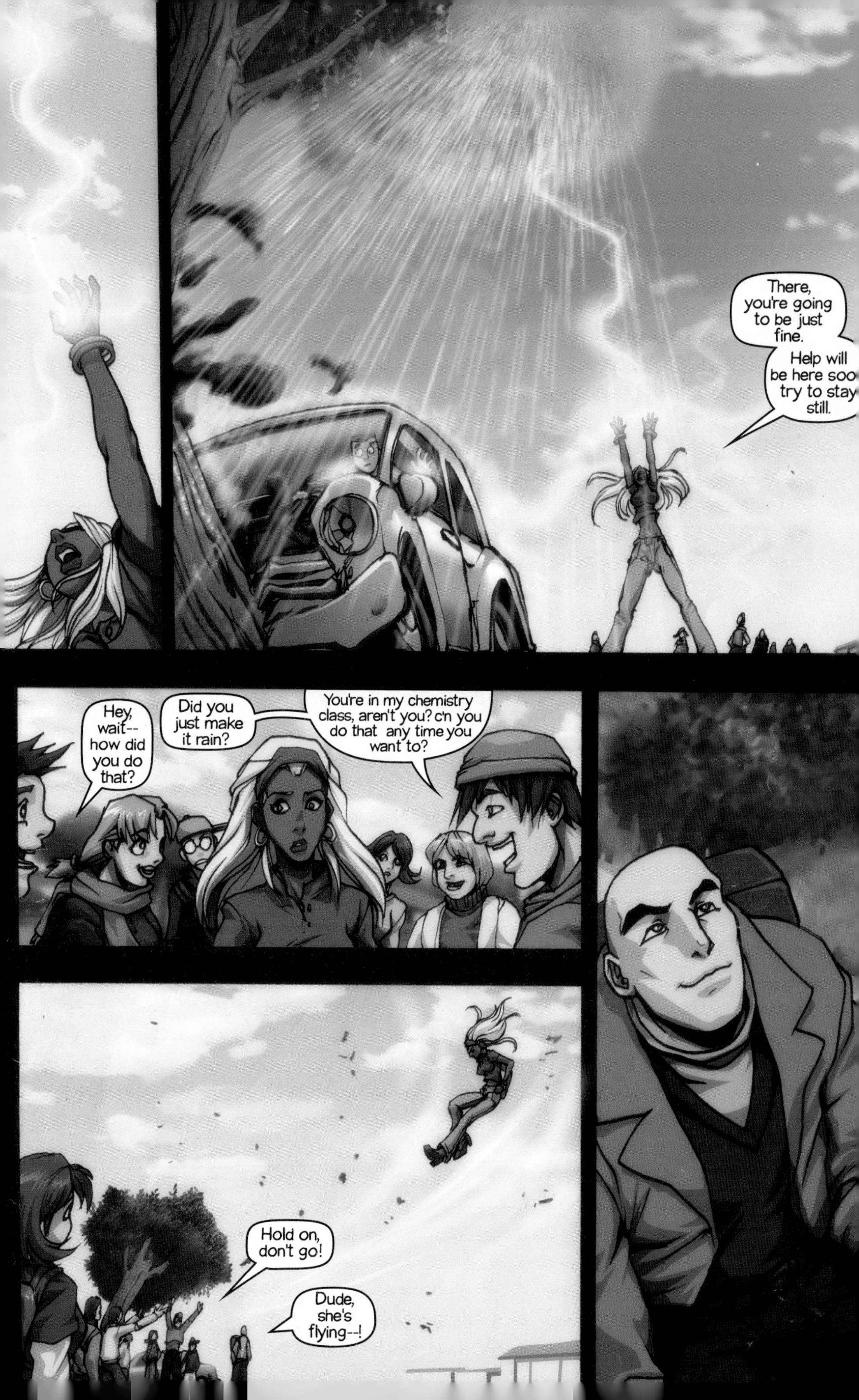
There, you're going to be just fine.
Help will be here soo try to stay still.
Hey, wait-- how did you do that?
Did you just make it rain?
You're in my chemistry class, aren't you? c'n you do that any time you want to?
Hold on, don't go!
Dude, she's flying--!

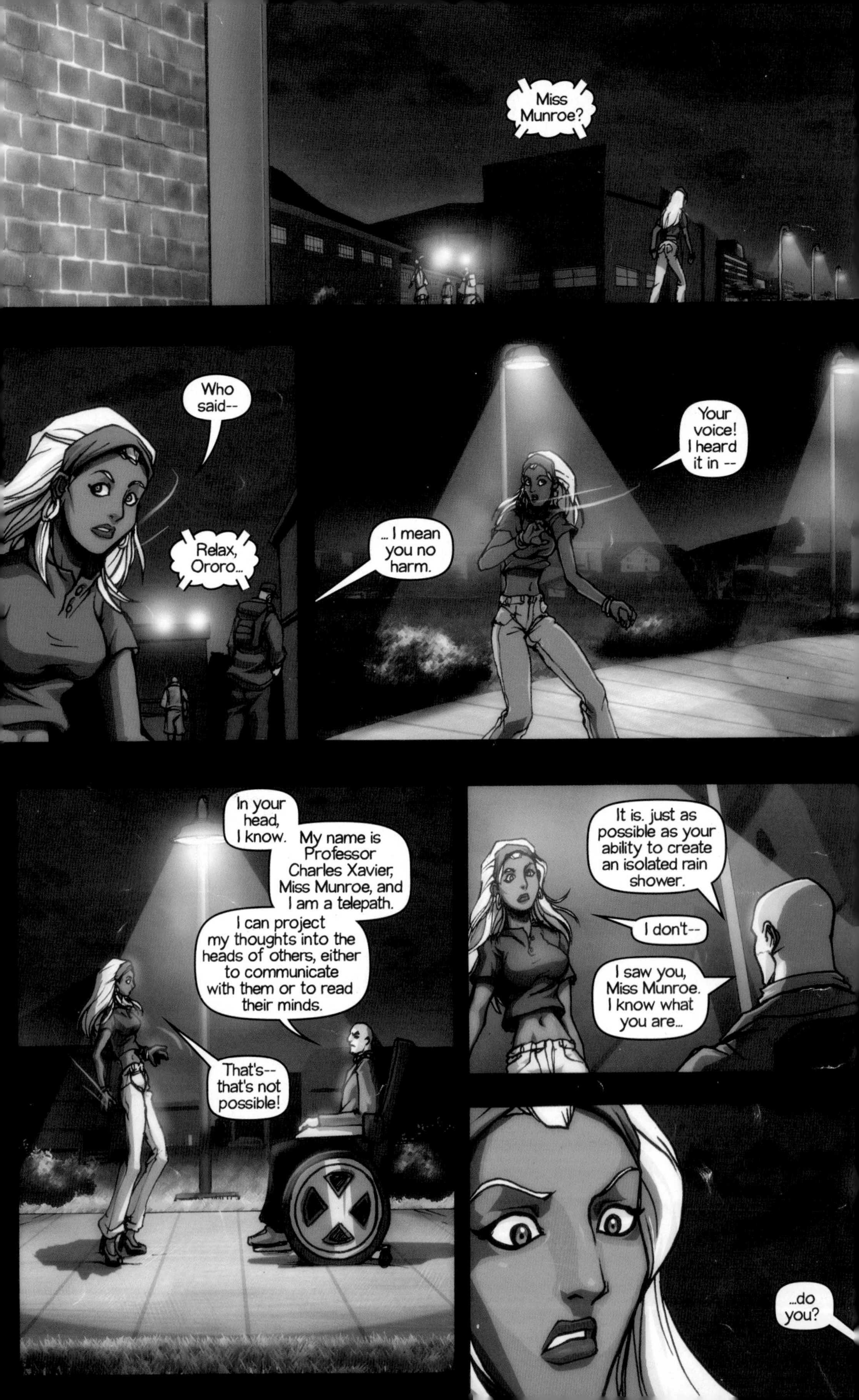
Miss Munroe?
Who said--
Relax, Ororo...
Your voice! I heard it in --
... I mean you no harm.
In your head, I know.
My name is Professor Charles Xavier, Miss Munroe, and I am a telepath.
I can project my thoughts into the heads of others, either to communicate with them or to read their minds.
That's-- that's not possible!
It is. just as possible as your ability to create an isolated rain shower.
I don't--
I saw you, Miss Munroe. I know what you are...
...do you?

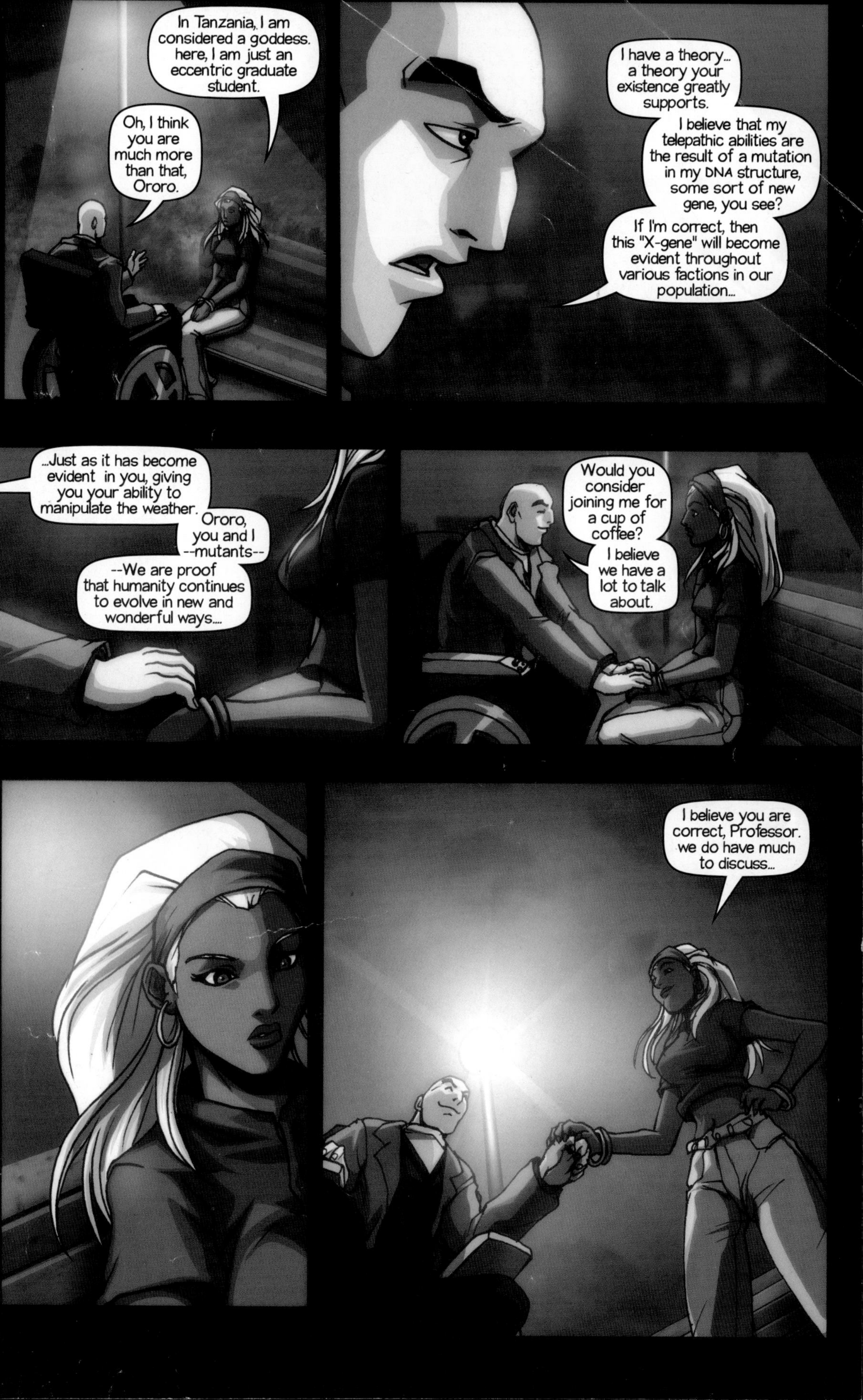

In Tanzania, I am considered a goddess. here, I am just an eccentric graduate student.
Oh, I think you are much more than that, Ororo.
I have a theory... a theory your existence greatly supports.
I believe that my telepathic abilities are the result of a mutation in my DNA structure, some sort of new gene, you see?
If I'm correct, then this "X-gene" will become evident throughout various factions in our population...
...Just as it has become evident in you, giving you your ability to manipulate the weather.
Ororo, you and I --mutants--
--We are proof that humanity continues to evolve in new and wonderful ways....
Would you consider joining me for a cup of coffee?
I believe we have a lot to talk about.
I believe you are correct, Professor. we do have much to discuss...

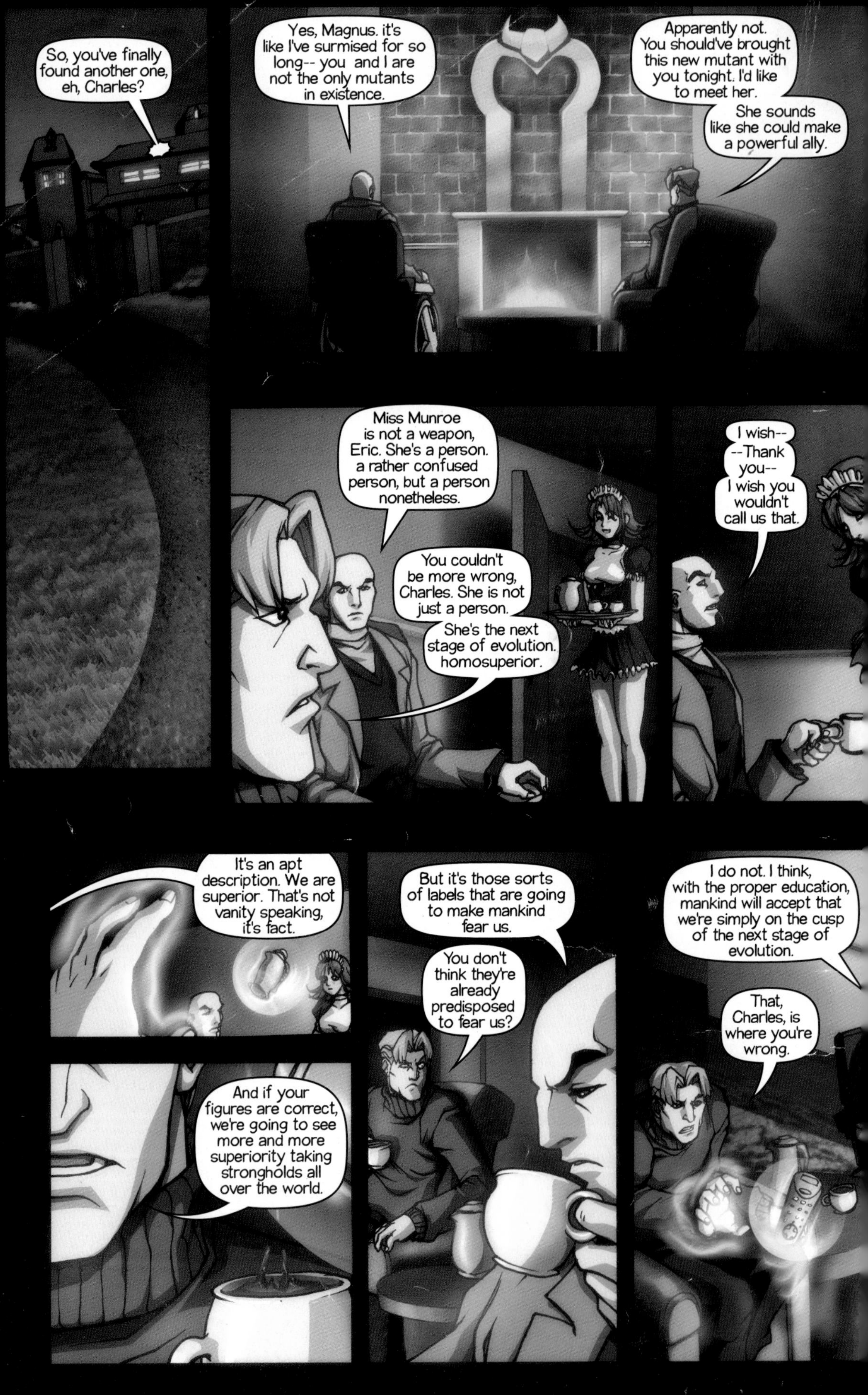
So, you've finally found another one, eh, Charles?
Yes, Magnus. it's like I've surmised for so long-- you and I are not the only mutants in existence.
Apparently not. You should've brought this new mutant with you tonight. I'd like to meet her.
She sounds like she could make a powerful ally.
Miss Munroe is not a weapon, Eric. She's a person. a rather confused person, but a person nonetheless.
You couldn't be more wrong, Charles. She is not just a person.
She's the next stage of evolution. homosuperior.
I wish--
--Thank you--
I wish you wouldn't call us that.
It's an apt description. We are superior. That's not vanity speaking, it's fact.
And if your figures are correct, we're going to see more and more superiority taking strongholds all over the world.
But it's those sorts of labels that are going to make mankind fear us.
You don't think they're already predisposed to fear us?
I do not. I think, with the proper education, mankind will accept that we're simply on the cusp of the next stage of evolution.
That, Charles, is where you're wrong.

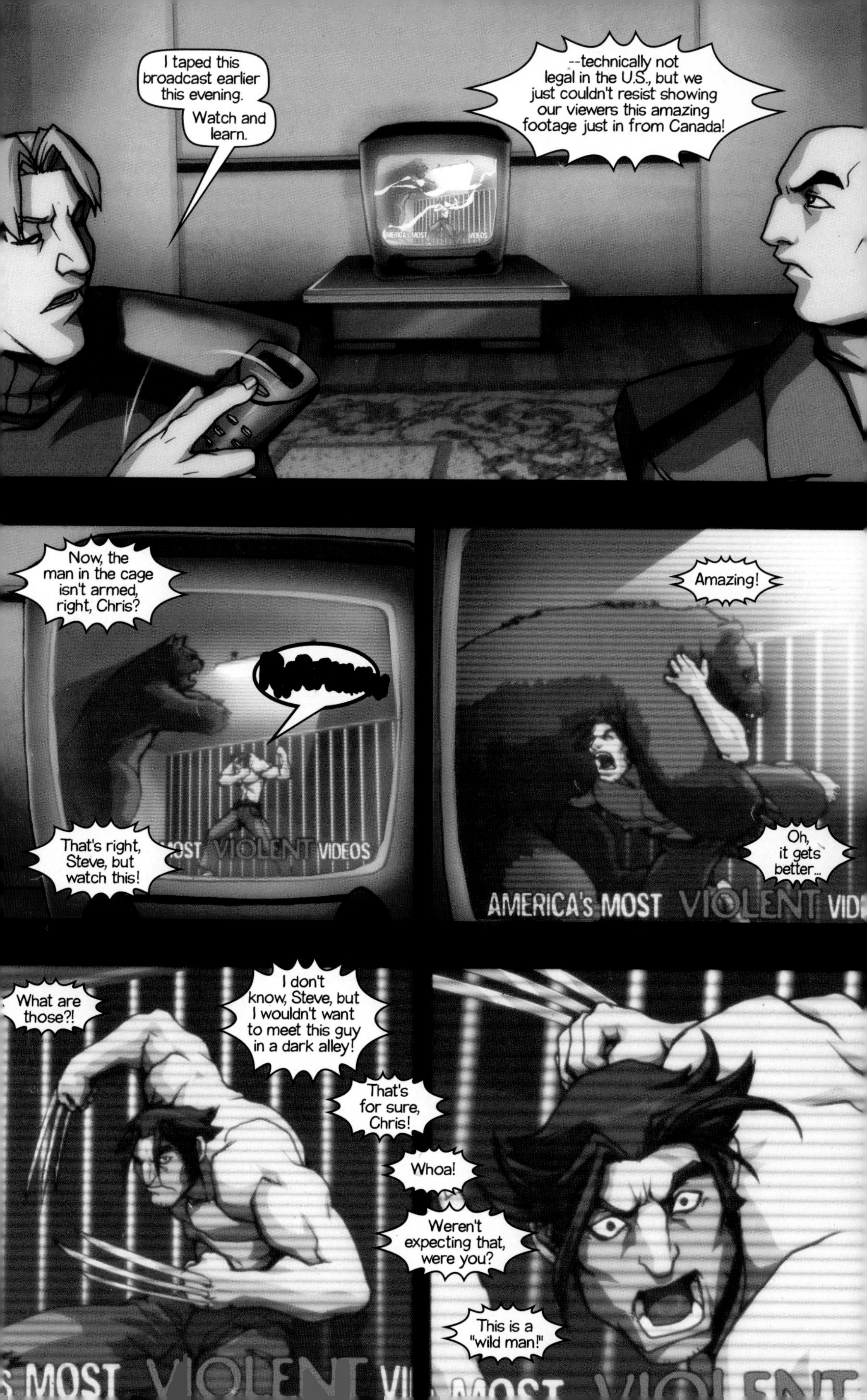
I taped this broadcast earlier this evening.
Watch and learn.
--technically not legal in the U.S., but we just couldn't resist showing our viewers this amazing footage just in from Canada!
AMERICA's MOST VIOLENT VIDEOS
Now, the man in the cage isn't armed, right, Chris?
That's right, Steve, but watch this!
MOST VIOLENT VIDEOS
Amazing!
Oh, it gets better...
AMERICA's MOST VIOLENT VID
What are those?!
I don't know, Steve, but I wouldn't want to meet this guy in a dark alley!
That's for sure, Chris!
Whoa!
Weren't expecting that, were you?
This is a "wild man!"
S MOST VIOLENT VI
MOST VIOLENT

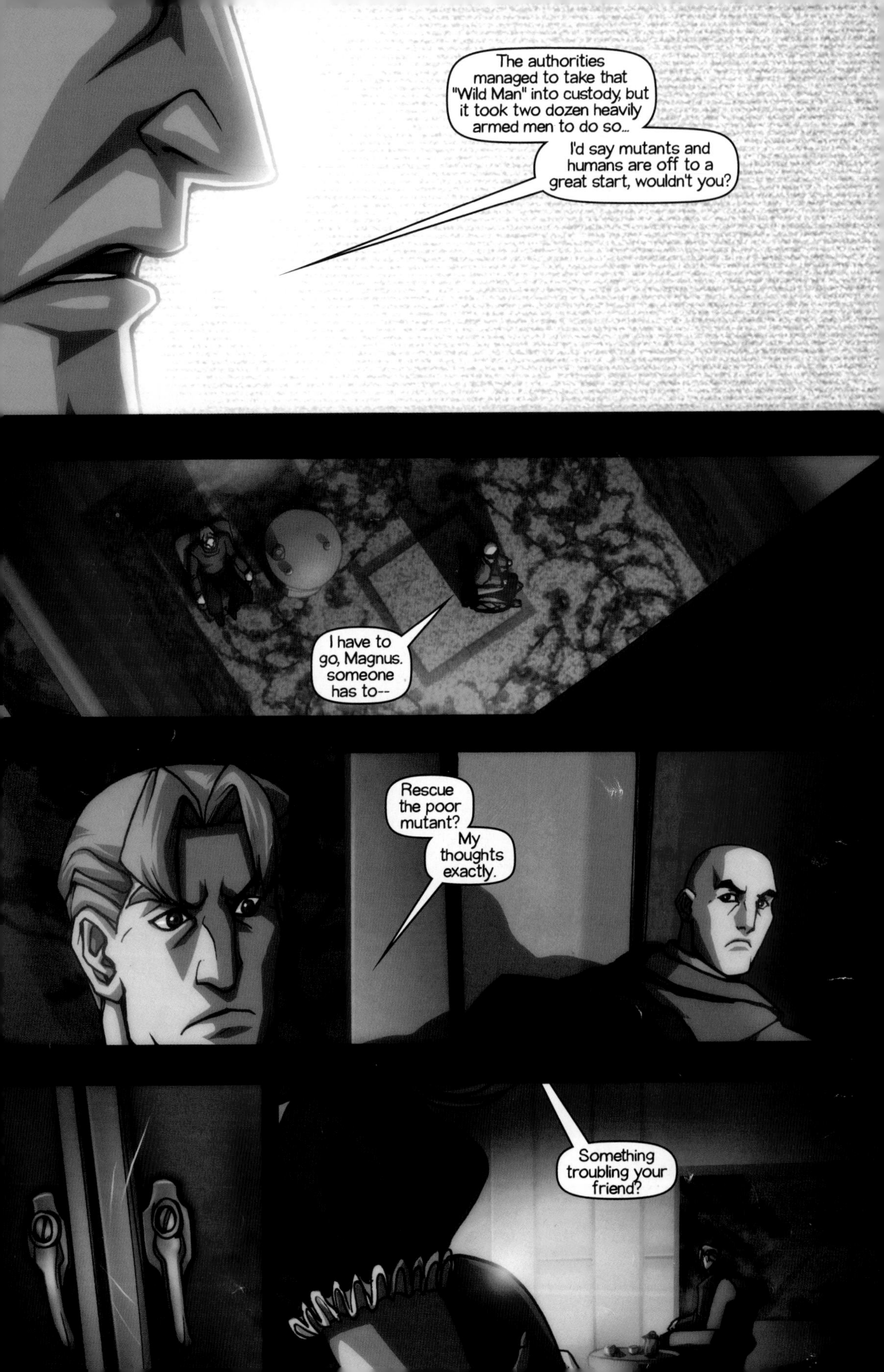
The authorities managed to take that "Wild Man" into custody, but it took two dozen heavily armed men to do so...
I'd say mutants and humans are off to a great start, wouldn't you?
I have to go, Magnus. someone has to--
Rescue the poor mutant?
My thoughts exactly.
Something troubling your friend?

He has a chronic case of idealism, that's all....

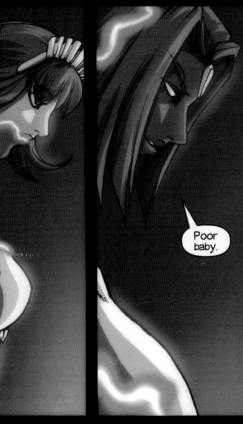

Poor baby.

I hope you don't mind, but I chose not to tell him about you just yet, Mystique....

Afraid it might be contagious?

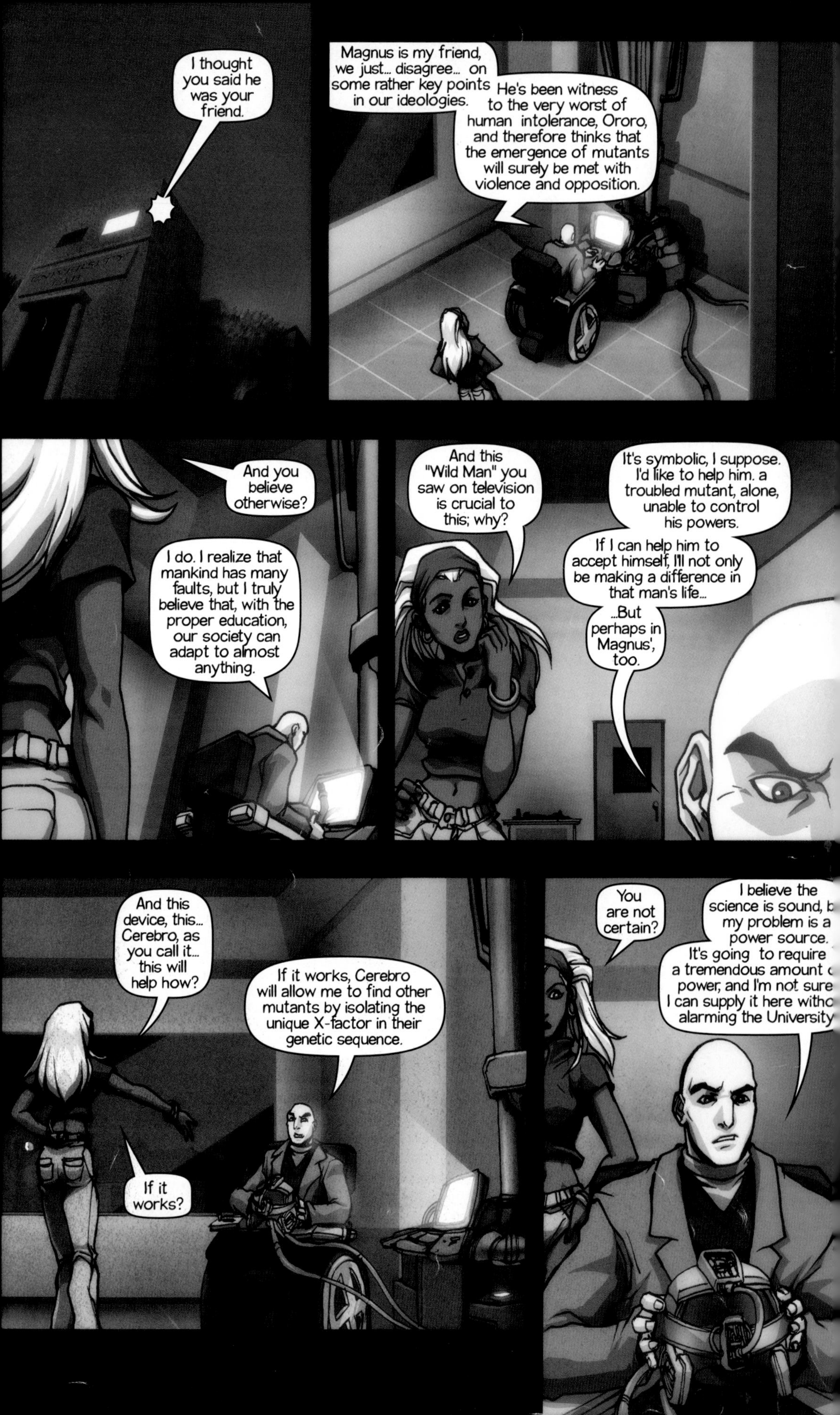
I thought you said he was your friend.
Magnus is my friend, we just... disagree... on some rather key points in our ideologies.
He's been witness to the very worst of human intolerance, Ororo, and therefore thinks that the emergence of mutants will surely be met with violence and opposition.
And you believe otherwise?
I do. I realize that mankind has many faults, but I truly believe that, with the proper education, our society can adapt to almost anything.
And this "Wild Man" you saw on television is crucial to this; why?
It's symbolic, I suppose. I'd like to help him. a troubled mutant, alone, unable to control his powers.
If I can help him to accept himself, I'll not only be making a difference in that man's life...
...But perhaps in Magnus', too.
And this device, this... Cerebro, as you call it... this will help how?
If it works, Cerebro will allow me to find other mutants by isolating the unique X-factor in their genetic sequence.
If it works?
You are not certain?
I believe the science is sound, b my problem is a power source. It's going to require a tremendous amount c power, and I'm not sure I can supply it here witho alarming the University

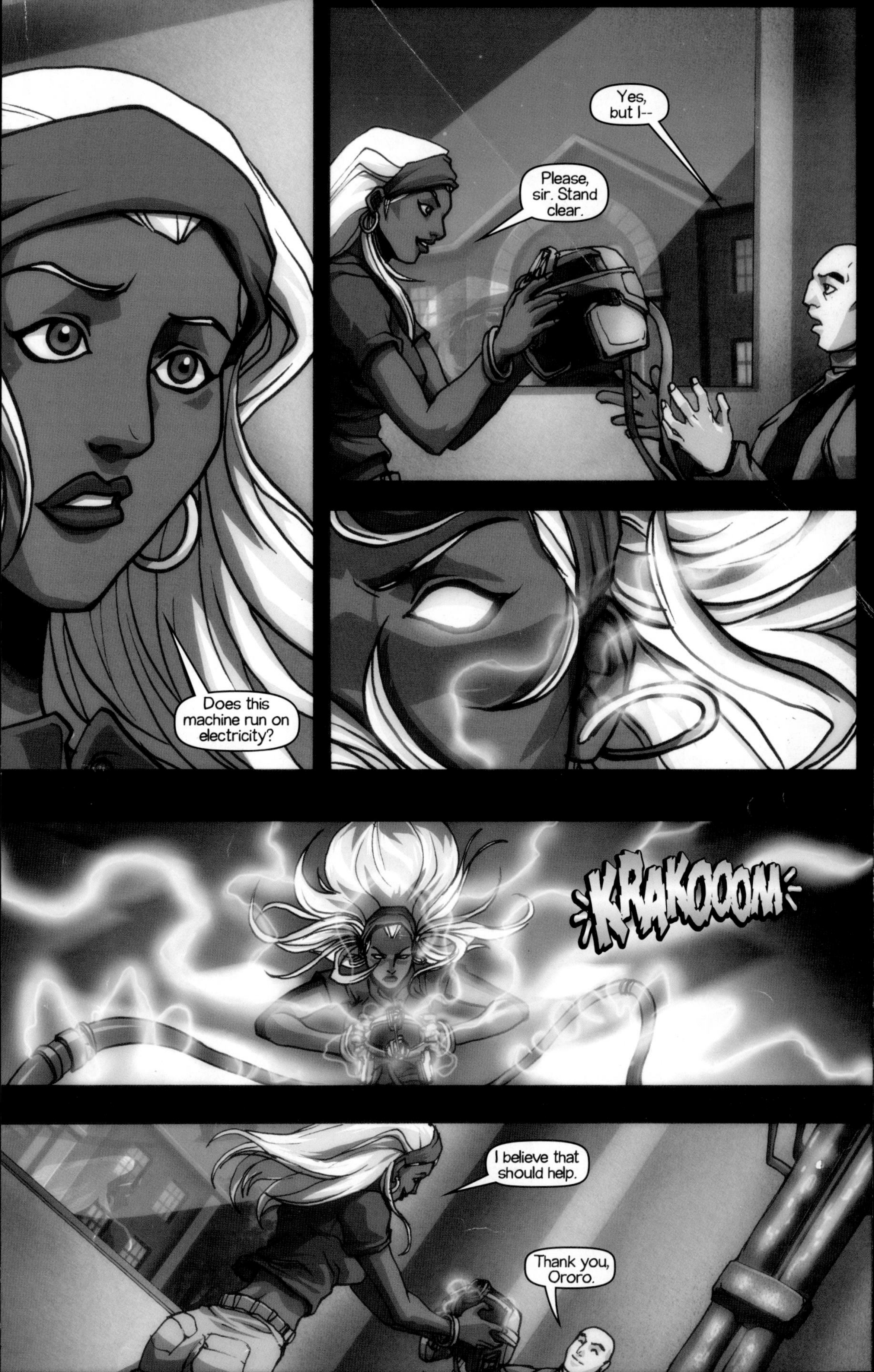

Does this machine run on electricity?
Yes, but I--
Please, sir. Stand clear.
KRAKOOOM
I believe that should help.
Thank you, Ororo.

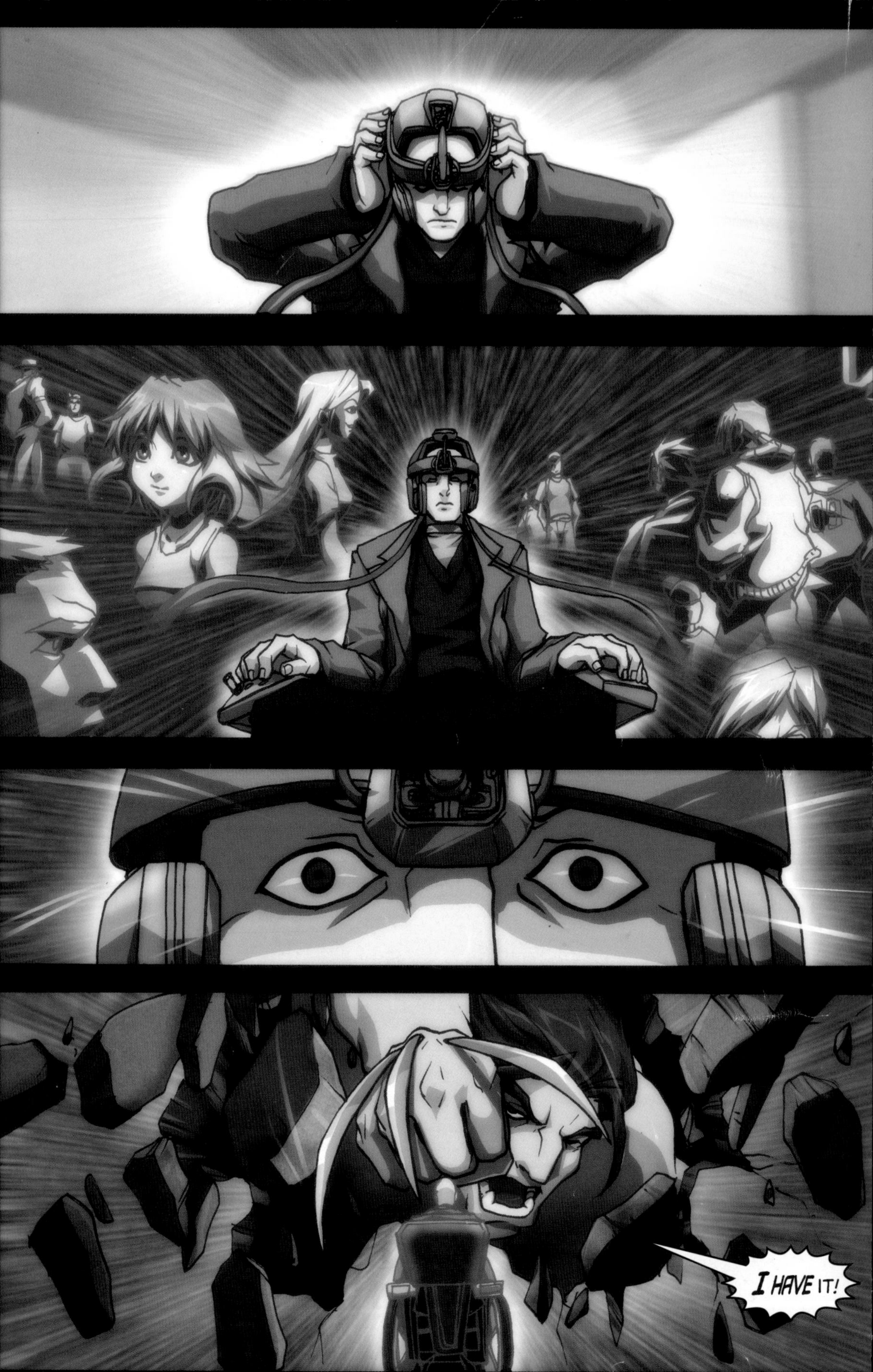
I HAVE IT!

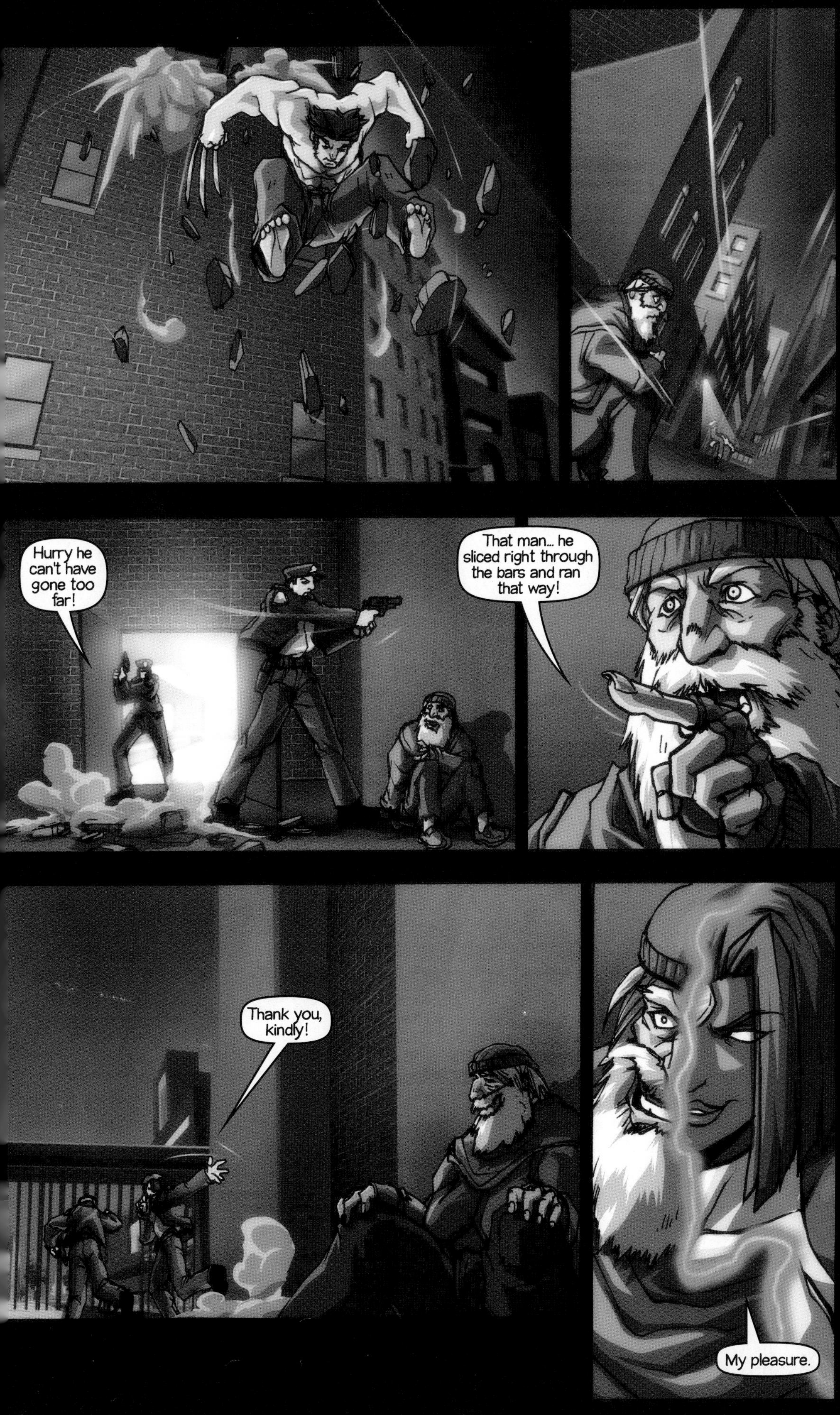
Hurry he can't have gone too far!
That man... he sliced right through the bars and ran that way!
Thank you, kindly!
My pleasure.

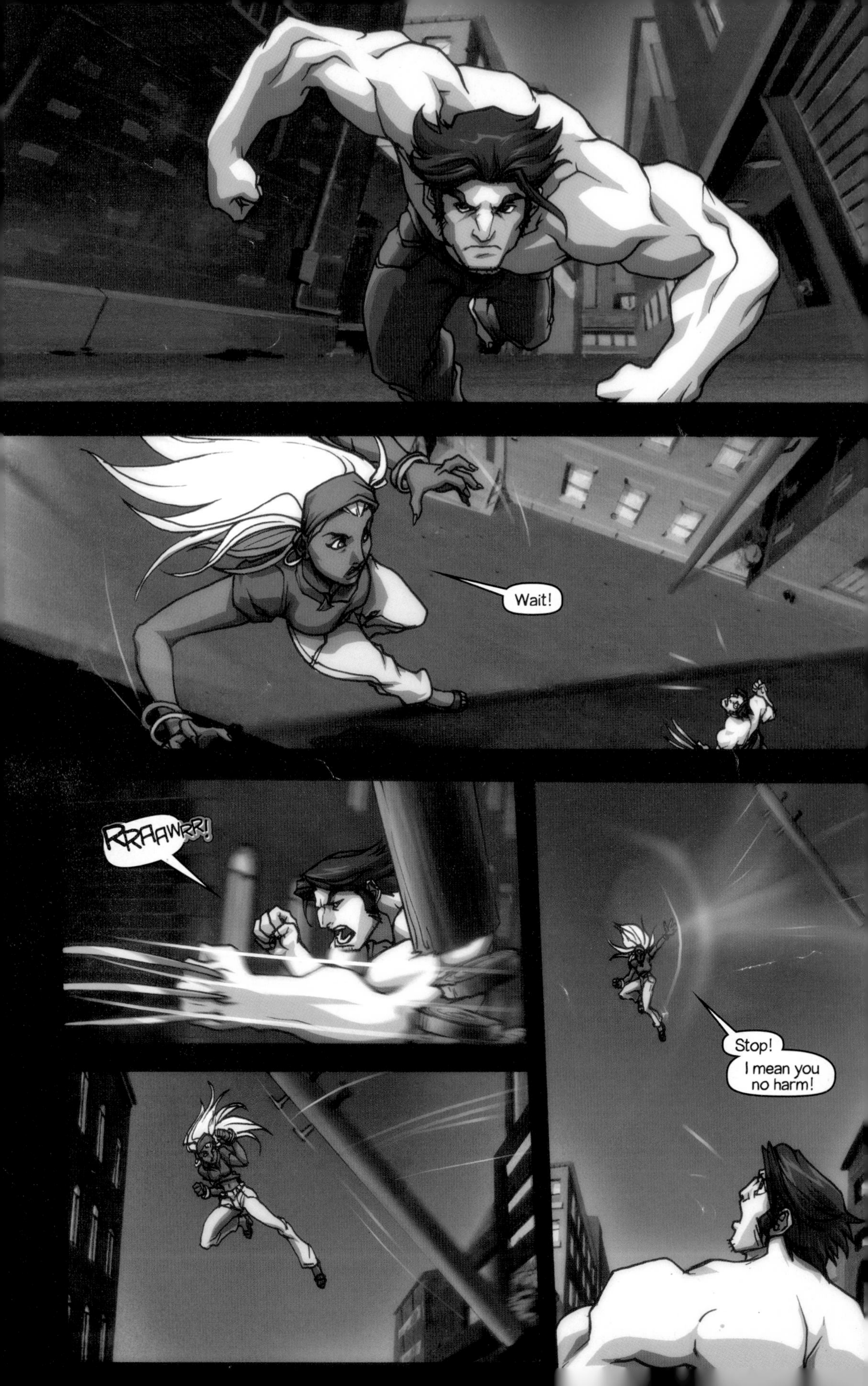
Wait!
RRAAWRR!
Stop!
I mean you no harm!

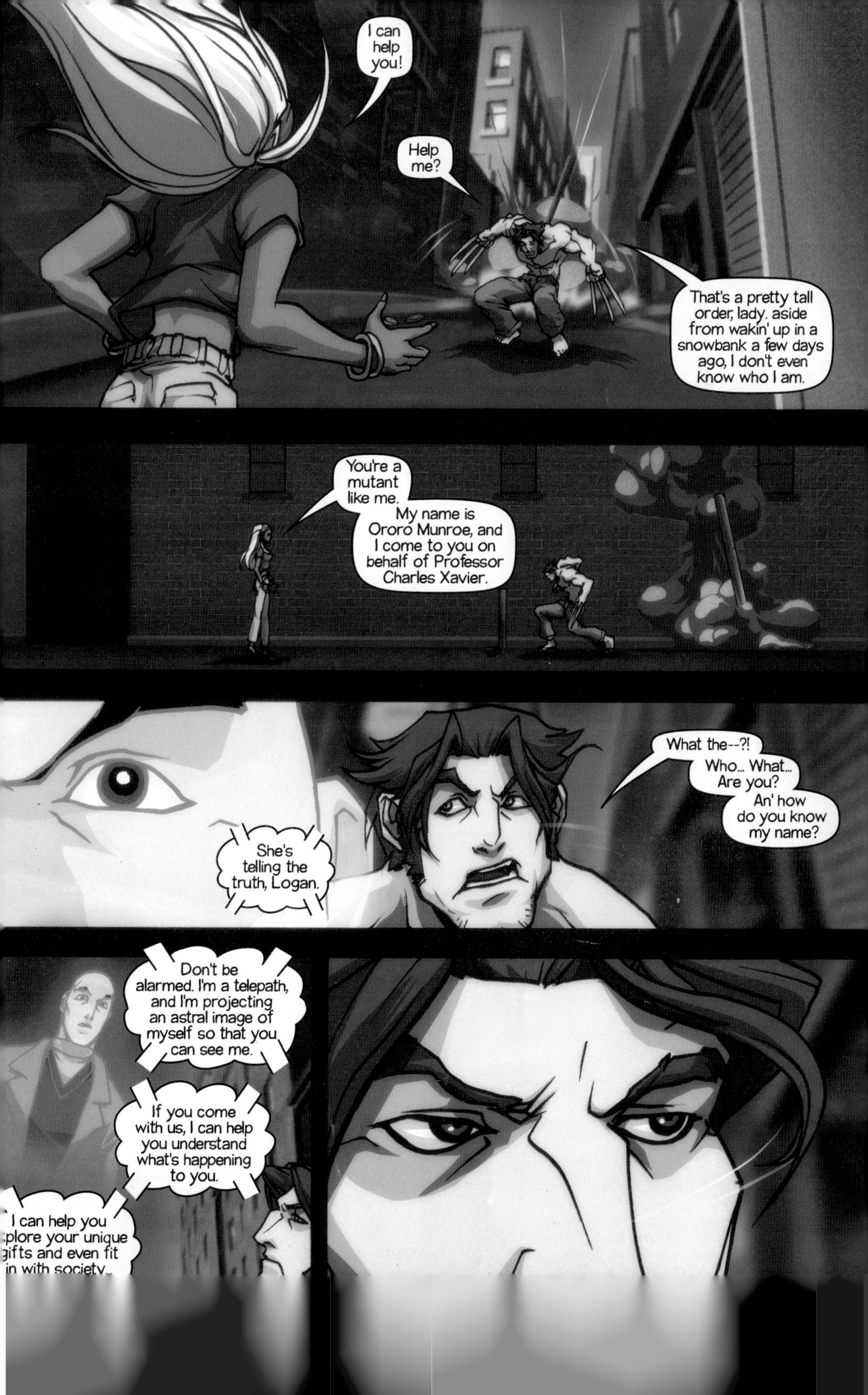
I can help you!
Help me?
That's a pretty tall order, lady. aside from wakin' up in a snowbank a few days ago, I don't even know who I am.
You're a mutant like me.
My name is Ororo Munroe, and I come to you on behalf of Professor Charles Xavier.
She's telling the truth, Logan.
What the--?!
Who... What... Are you?
An' how do you know my name?
Don't be alarmed. I'm a telepath, and I'm projecting an astral image of myself so that you can see me.
If you come with us, I can help you understand what's happening to you.
I can help you splore your unique gifts and even fit in with society...

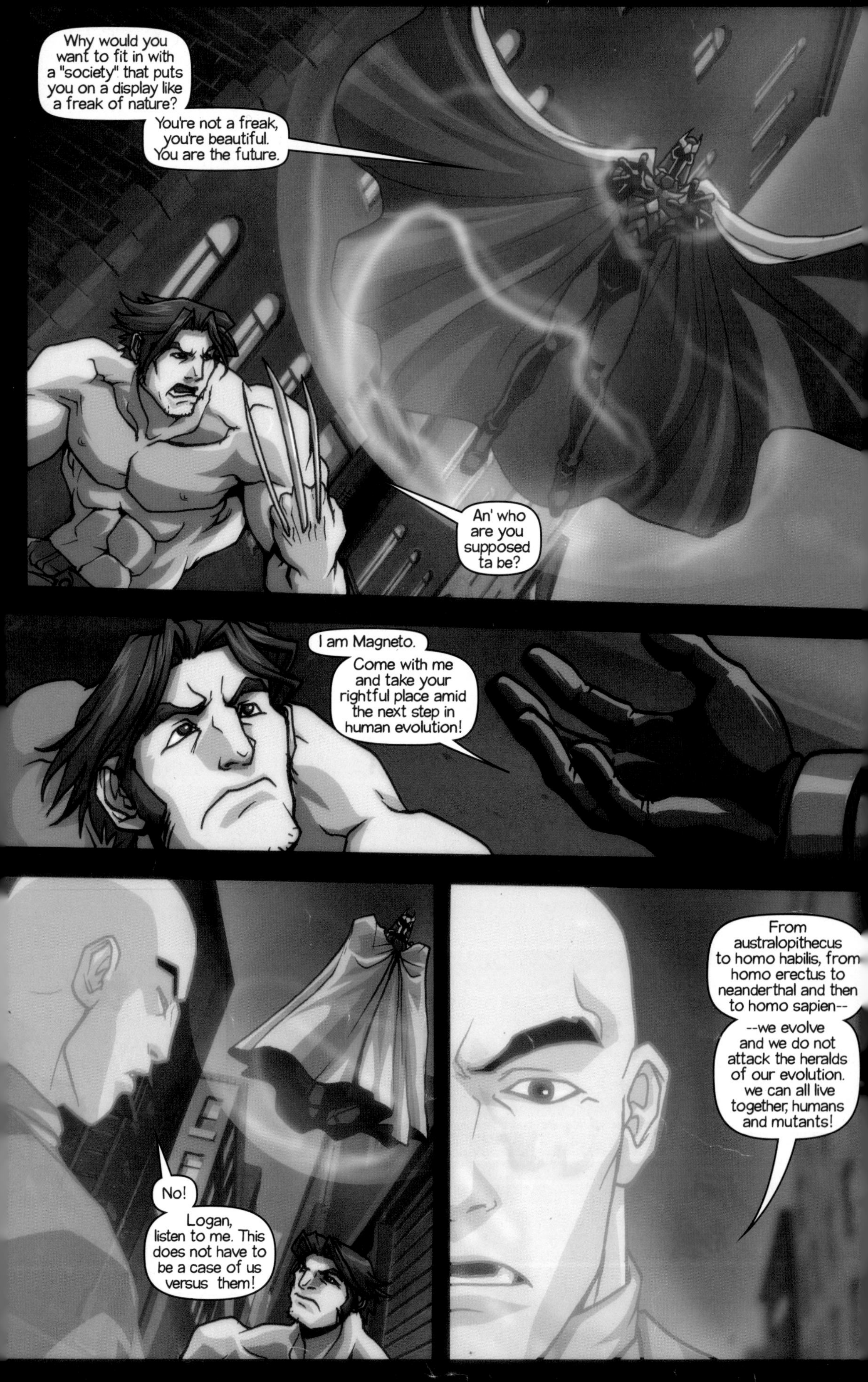
Why would you want to fit in with a "society" that puts you on a display like a freak of nature?
You're not a freak, you're beautiful. You are the future.
An' who are you supposed ta be?
I am Magneto.
Come with me and take your rightful place amid the next step in human evolution!
No!
Logan, listen to me. This does not have to be a case of us versus them!
From australopithecus to homo habilis, from homo erectus to neanderthal and then to homo sapien--
--we evolve and we do not attack the heralds of our evolution. we can all live together, humans and mutants!

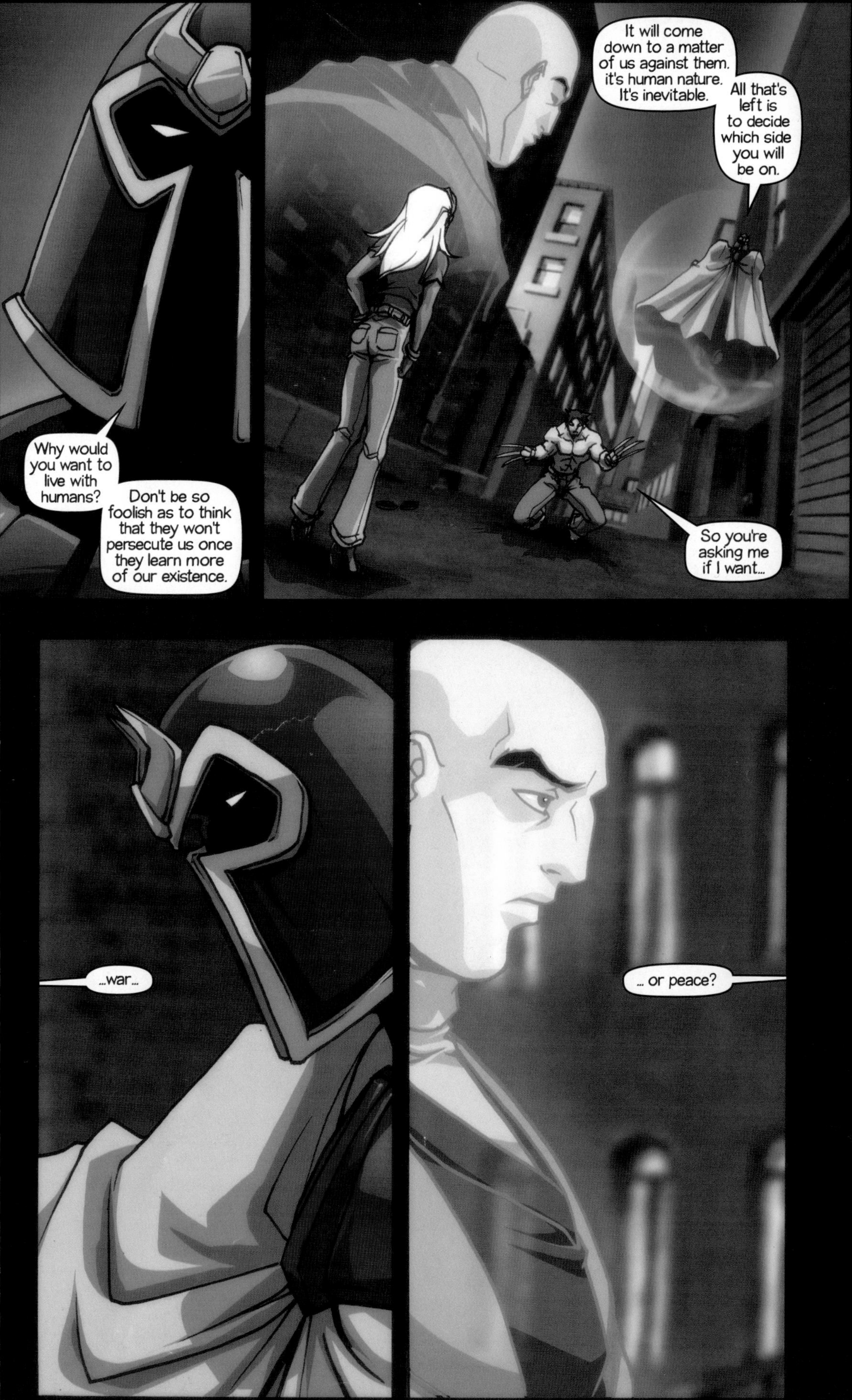
Why would you want to live with humans?
Don't be so foolish as to think that they won't persecute us once they learn more of our existence.
It will come down to a matter of us against them. it's human nature. It's inevitable.
All that's left is to decide which side you will be on.
So you're asking me if I want...
...war...
... or peace?

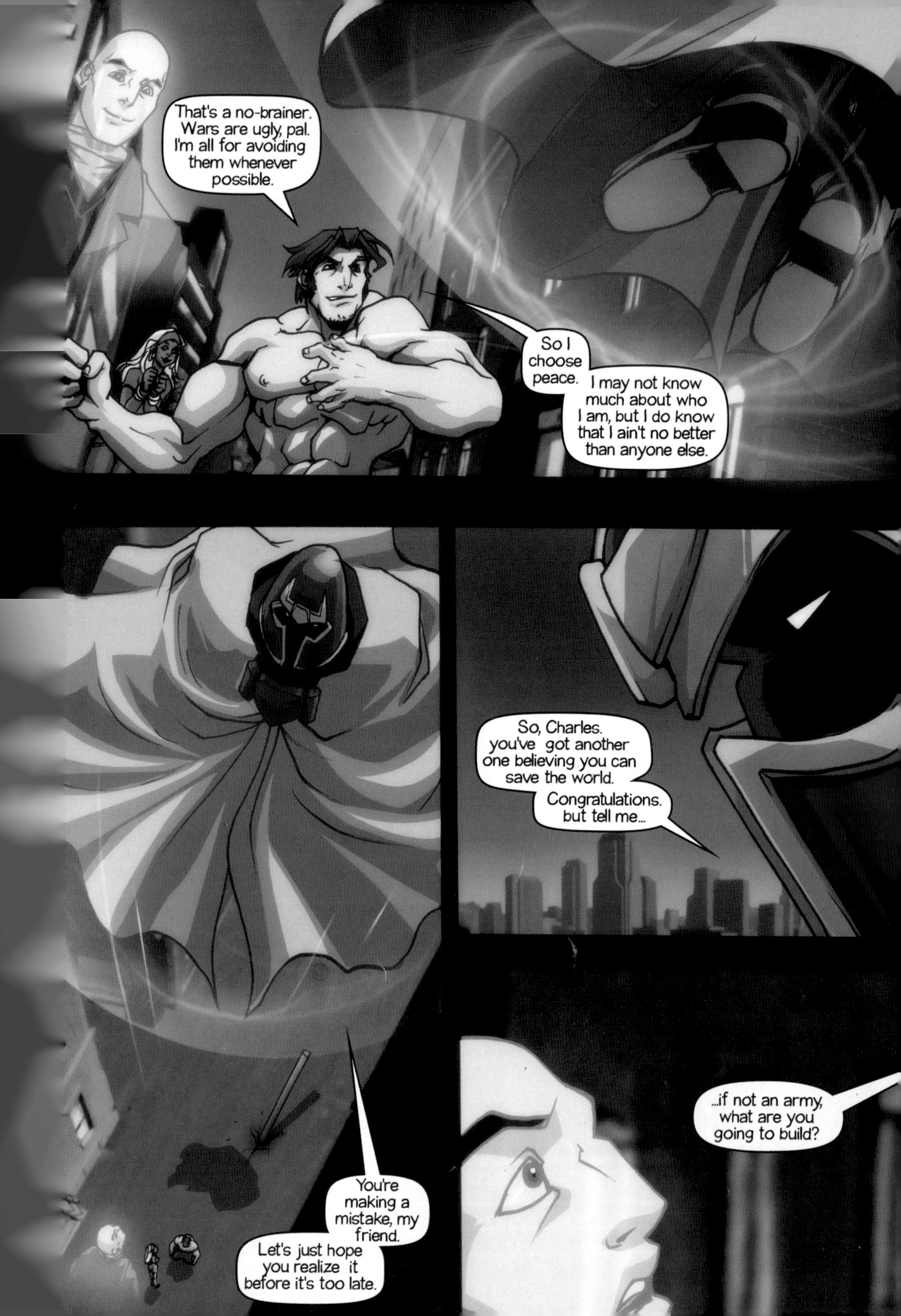
That's a no-brainer. Wars are ugly, pal. I'm all for avoiding them whenever possible.
So I choose peace.
I may not know much about who I am, but I do know that I ain't no better than anyone else.
So, Charles. you've got another one believing you can save the world.
Congratulations. but tell me...
...if not an army, what are you going to build?
You're making a mistake, my friend.
Let's just hope you realize it before it's too late.

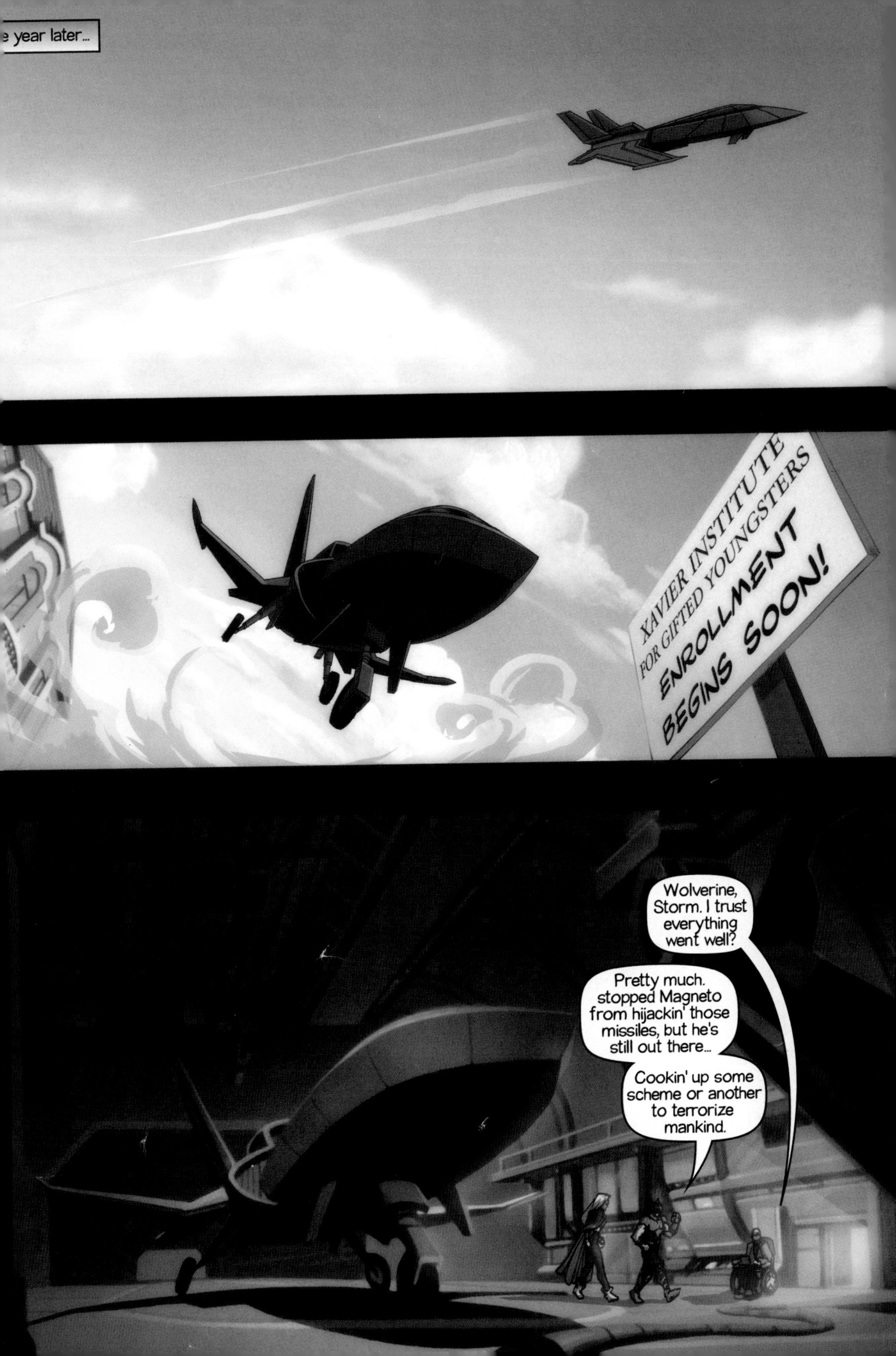
e year later...
XAVIER INSTITUTE
FOR GIFTED YOUNGSTERS
ENROLLMENT BEGINS SOON!
Wolverine, Storm. I trust everything went well?
Pretty much. stopped Magneto from hijackin' those missiles, but he's still out there...
Cookin' up some scheme or another to terrorize mankind.

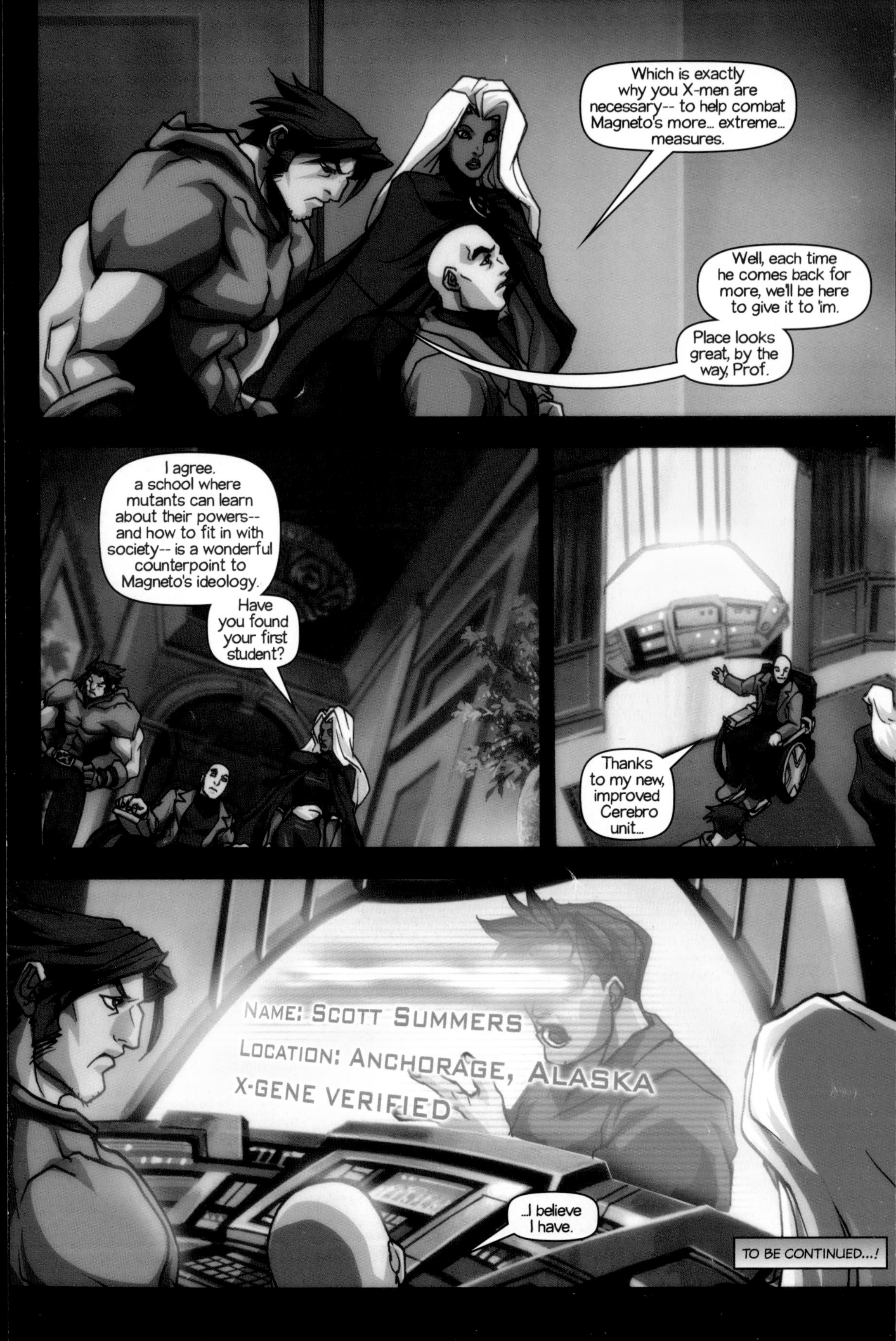
Which is exactly why you X-men are necessary-- to help combat Magneto's more... extreme... measures.
Well, each time he comes back for more, we'll be here to give it to 'im.
Place looks great, by the way, Prof.
I agree. a school where mutants can learn about their powers-- and how to fit in with society-- is a wonderful counterpoint to Magneto's ideology.
Have you found your first student?
Thanks to my new, improved Cerebro unit...
NAME: SCOTT SUMMERS
LOCATION: ANCHORAGE, ALASKA
X-GENE VERIFIED
...I believe I have.
TO BE CONTINUED...!